KYLE MEWBURN • DONOVAN

DinoSaur Trouble

The Lava Melt Shake

SCHOLASTIC

AUCKLAND SYDNEY NEW YORK LONDON TORONTO
MEXICO CITY NEW DELHI HONG KONG

First published in 2017 by Scholastic New Zealand Limited
Private Bag 94407, Botany, Auckland 2163, New Zealand

Scholastic Australia Pty Limited
PO Box 579, Gosford, NSW 2250, Australia

Text © Kyle Mewburn, 2017
Illustrations © Donovan Bixley, 2017

ISBN 978-1-77543-367-5

A catalogue record for this book is available from the National Library of New Zealand.

---

12 11 10 9 8 7 6 5 4 3 2 1   7 8 9 / 1

Publishing team: Lynette Evans, Penny Scown and Sophia Broom
Cover design by Steve Wells
Design and layup by Donovan Bixley, Magma Design
Typeset in Berkeley Oldstyle
Printed by McPherson's Printing Group, Maryborough, Victoria, Australia

Scholastic New Zealand's policy is to use papers that are renewable and made efficiently
from wood grown in responsibly managed forests, so as to minimise its environmental
footprint.

For Jules — K.M.

For Simon Kirkland — D.B.

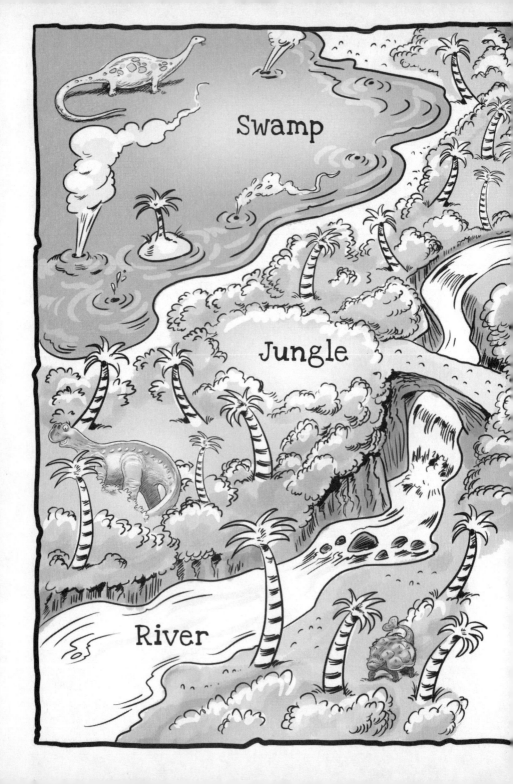

Chapter 1

Oh no! The volcano is erupting! Everything is shaking. The ground is shaking. The cliffs are shaking. The jungle is shaking.

Everyone in the tribe is shaking, too. They are very, VERY scared.

There are seven reasons why everyone is so scared:

1. Huge boulders keep tumbling down the cliffs. It is very dangerous to be outside. But inside is not much safer. The caves might collapse and bury them alive.

2. A river of red-hot lava is heading straight for the village. It is so hot that the jungle is bursting into flames. If it cannot be stopped, the tribe will have to run away. Living beside a lava river is much too dangerous. Especially if you sleepwalk.

3. The volcano has filled the valley with thick smoke and soot. It is very hard to breathe. Worse, it makes their snot black and crunchy. Crunchy black snot tastes terrible.

4. The smoke is so thick that the lookouts cannot see anything. The Grogllgrox could launch a surprise attack anytime. They live in the next valley and are a very nasty tribe.

5. The eruption is scaring away the dinosaurs. If it does not stop soon, everyone will have only cycad roots to eat. Cycad roots taste worse than crunchy black snot.

6. If the lava destroys the jungle, they will not even have cycad roots to eat. Instead, they will have a terrible choice: stay and starve, or run away and face the fearsome Grogllgrox.

7. Cave people think the number 7 is very unlucky. So having 7 reasons to be scared makes everyone extra scared. (Note: Today, some people think 13 is unlucky. But cave people can't count past 10.)

The hunters are trying to stop the lava river. Arg wants to help, but his mum says it is too dangerous.

She says he has to stay on his bed rock until the eruption stops.

Arg always tries to do as he's told. But sometimes it's impossible.

For a start, his bed rock is shaking so much, it keeps throwing him off.

So he draws dinosaurs on his
wall instead. But everything is shaking
so hard, his drawings look more like
dinosaur poos with legs.

A loud rumbling fills the cave. It sounds like a grumbling T-rex tummy. A volcano is a bit like a starving T-rex. It is very angry and wants to eat everything in its path. Except a volcano is a lot scarier. T-rexes do not fart hot gas or belch lava. And you can't stop a volcano with a spear.

Arg imagines the hunters attacking the lava with their spears. Cave people are not very smart sometimes. But Arg's big brain is always coming up with clever ideas. He might be able to help.

He sneaks past his mum and rushes outside.

Chapter 2

Arg finds the hunters beside the river of lava. It is destroying everything in its path. Trees burst into flame. The air is thick with choking smoke. It is so hot it feels like Arg's face is melting.

The hunters look very scared. They all want to run away. Nobody has ever stopped lava before. But if they run away, the village will be destroyed.

Two hunters leap up and down. They wave their spears and yell loudly. Maybe they can scare the lava away? It works for T-rexes . . . sometimes. (Though 'sometimes' sort of means 'hardly ever'. Mostly they just get eaten. Actually it *never* works and they *always* get eaten. So ignore that bit.)

With a fierce screech, one hunter
leaps forward. He jabs the lava with
his spear! The flint spearhead glows
orange for a second … then melts.

The shaft bursts into flames and
the hunter squeals. He tumbles
backwards as the ground turns into
lava beneath his feet.

Arg's dad is staring into the lava. He is scratching his head, trying to figure out what to do. Arg thinks his dad will be happy to see him. But he is not happy at *all*. In fact, he is the total opposite.

"Arg go!" he shouts. At least that is what Arg *thinks* he says. He can't be sure because the roaring of the burning trees is deafening.

"Maybe I can help!" Arg yells back.

Arg's dad yells something else. But it is drowned out by a loud **CRACK!**

Then a terrible WH-O-O-O-O-SH
sound slices the air. A huge, flaming
tree is hurtling straight towards them.

The hunters scatter. They are
hooting and hollering as if they have
been bitten on the bottom
by a velociraptor.

But Arg's feet stay rooted to the spot. He cannot move! He makes a face and throws one arm up.

CRASH

Just in time, Arg's dad snatches him up. He leaps clear as the tree crashes to the ground. Then he sprints through the jungle, with Arg bobbing wildly in his arms.

Arg's dad does not slow down until they are halfway back to the village. Finally, he drops Arg to the ground. Arg thinks he will be angry. But he's not. He is just very scared.

"Arg go," he says. He gives Arg a gentle push, then turns back. His shoulders are slumped. Arg can tell that he is not sure he can beat the lava.

There is no way Arg is going to let his dad face the lava alone. His dad is the strongest and bravest hunter in the village. But sometimes a big brain is more useful than big muscles.

As soon as his dad is out of sight, Arg follows him.

Chapter 3

Halfway back, Arg hears a strange sound. *Snort ... scrape ... stomp ... grunt, grunt.*

It doesn't sound dangerous. But he is not taking any chances. It would be embarrassing to be the first person eaten by a weird new dinosaur. And it would be pretty selfish to get eaten when nobody else was around to see. Cave people learn a lot from other cave people's mistakes. That is how they found out which berries were poisonous. And why it was never a good idea to leave a rotting dinosaur too close to the fire.

Arg tiptoes along a narrow path. The sound gets louder. And louder.

Snort ... scrape ... stomp ... grunt, grunt. Snort ... scrape ... stomp ... grunt, grunt.

It is very close now.

He slips his hands between the
fronds of a giant fern. Then, holding
his breath, he eases them apart . . .

Arg's mouth gapes open.

A HUGE triceratops is staring right back at him.

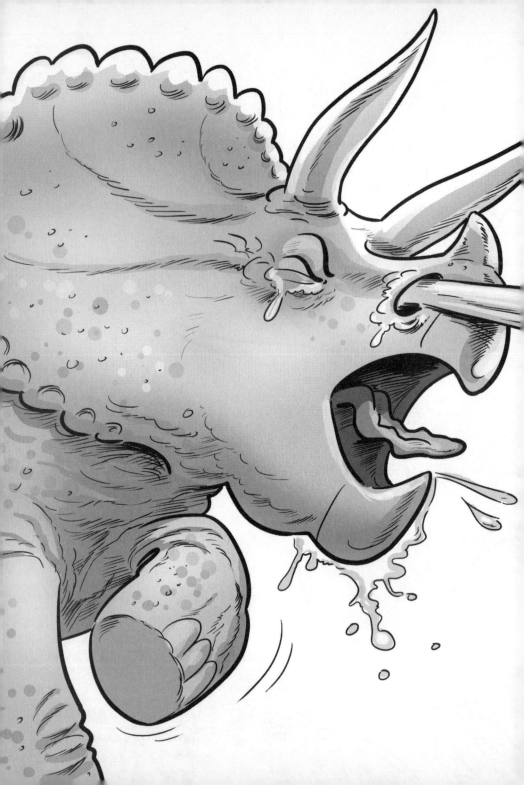

SNORT!

A jet of cold triceratops snot sprays Arg's face. His mouth snaps shut just in time.

The triceratops bows its head.
Drool and snot spill from its snout.
It scrapes its massive horns along the
ground. It stumbles forward, then
stomps its hoof.

Arg has never seen a triceratops acting so strangely. Is it sick?

When he hears grunting, Arg smiles. He recognises the sound right away. His head whips around.

Aha! He spots Shlok, perched
on a rock. Shlok is Arg's best friend.
They are exactly the same age. Arg is
much smarter, but Shlok is a genius at
getting into trouble.

That is why they are best friends.

Arg has saved Shlok's life hundreds of times. But Shlok has saved Arg just as many times. A big brain doesn't always stop you doing dumb things.

Shlok is holding a long feather.

"What are you doing, Shlok?" Arg hisses.

"Shhhhh," says Shlok, holding his finger to his lips.

He slips the feather under the triceratops and wiggles it along its belly.

The triceratops shakes its head
wildly, snorting snot everywhere.
Then its sharp horns scrape along
the ground.

Shlok stops tickling, and the
triceratops stumbles forward.
It stomps a heavy hoof.

Then it goes right back to grazing.
Triceratops have very short memories
and very big appetites.

Shlok laughs. Arg laughs too.
Triceratops have very tough skin.

Arg would never have guessed they were ticklish. Not in a million moons.

The ticklish triceratops has scraped a deep groove in the ground. It is almost as wide as the lava river . . .

Arg hurries to join Shlok.

He has a plan.

Chapter 4

Snort ... scrape ... stomp ... grunt, grunt. Snort ... scrape ... stomp ... grunt, grunt. Arg's plan is working.

Every time Shlok tickles the triceratops, the groove gets one step closer to the lava river. When they meet, the lava will change its path and flow safely away. At least that is what Arg *hopes* will happen.

They are close now. Arg can hear the lava bubbling. But it is taking way too long to reach it. Once the lava flows past, he won't be able to change its course.

They would go a lot faster if Shlok didn't keep stopping to laugh.

"Hurry up, Shlok," Arg grumbles.

"Tricep ... tricerta ... dinosaur

funny," Shlok grunts.

"Give me a go," says Arg, snatching at the feather.

"No. Feather Shlok!" Shlok growls, jerking away.

"I'm not going to keep it,"
says Arg. "I just want to —"

As Arg stretches for the feather
again, Shlok pushes him.

Arg squeals as he loses his balance.

It is only a short fall, but time enough for his big brain to imagine lots of terrible possibilities.

Like . . . his arms could snap in half and be as useless as a T-rex's.

Or his brain could get smashed and he will be dumber than an ankylosaur. Or he will get trampled by the triceratops.
Or speared by its horn.
Or maybe all of them together. Or . . .

He lands on the triceratops' back
with a THUMP.

The triceratops bolts ahead,
snorting in surprise.

It ploughs through the jungle,
trampling everything in its path.

Arg holds on tight. He isn't
relieved. Or even scared. He is too sad
to feel anything. His plan has failed.
Now the village will be destroyed.
Even worse, his dad is in danger.
He will risk his life to stop the lava
– and the lava will surely win.

The smoke is so thick it is like a
blindfold. But Arg is smart enough
to know that the rising heat and
deafening roar can only mean one
thing – they are heading straight for
the lava!

A wave of heat hits them. It is hot

enough to singe Arg's hair. So hot that
even the triceratops notices. It rears
up in fear then plants its front hooves.

It tries to swerve away, but is going much too fast. Its rump slides forward and slams into the base of a massive cycad.

The jolt throws Arg high into
the air.

The cycad wobbles ... then begins
to topple sideways.

The triceratops scrambles to its feet
and lumbers away.

Arg screams as he falls towards
the lava. The air is too hot to breathe.
His face feels like it's on fire.

He has to close his eyes to stop
them melting. This is going to hurt!
But at least it should be quick . . .
he hopes.

A sudden, painful jerk nearly tugs his arm loose. Then his feet hit solid ground. When he opens his eyes, he is not *too* surprised to see his dad grinning beside him.

"Good catch, Dad," says Arg.

RUMBLE RUMBLE

The ground starts moving beneath their feet. Uh-oh! The toppled cycad has loosened a rockslide. Boulders tumble down the mountain like a herd of somersaulting apatosaurs.

They race for their lives, dodging
and weaving. As they reach the safety
of a rocky outcrop, half the hillside
slips away. A deep gash slices right
across the lava's path. The lava oozes
down the gash, heading away.

The village is saved!

The hunters cheer. They think the rockslide was a lucky coincidence.

Only Arg's dad suspects that it wasn't. He is sure Arg had *something* to do with it. But his brain is too small to figure out what.

With a shrug, he lifts Arg onto his shoulders. It will be their little secret. Because if Arg's mum ever finds out, they'll both be in huge trouble.